Sports Superstars

Peyton Manning

Football Star

Mary Ann Hoffman

PowerKiDS
press.

New York

Published in 2007 by The Rosen Publishing Group, Inc.
29 East 21st Street, New York, NY 10010

Book Design: Daniel Hosek

Photo Credits: Cover © Nick Laham/Getty Images; pp. 5, 21 © Jonathan Daniel/Getty Images; p. 7 © Robert Laberge/Getty Images; pp. 9, 17 © Jamie Squire/Getty Images; p. 11 © Chris Trotman/Getty Images; p. 13 © Rick Stewart/Getty images; p. 15 © Streeter Lecka/Getty Images; p. 19 © Elsa/Getty Images.

Library of Congress Cataloging-in-Publication Data

Hoffman, Mary Ann, 1947-
  Peyton Manning : football star / Mary Ann Hoffman.
      p. cm. — (Sports superstars)
  Includes bibliographical references and index.
  ISBN-13: 978-1-4042-3531-0
  ISBN-10: 1-4042-3531-0
  1. Manning, Peyton—Juvenile literature. 2. Football players—United States—Biography—Juvenile literature. I. Title.
  GV939.M289H64 2007
  796.332092—dc22
  (B)
                                    2006014640

Manufactured in the United States of America

Contents

Peyton Manning is a great quarterback. He plays for the Indianapolis Colts.

5

Peyton threw forty-nine touchdown passes in 2004. No one else has ever thrown that many in 1 year!

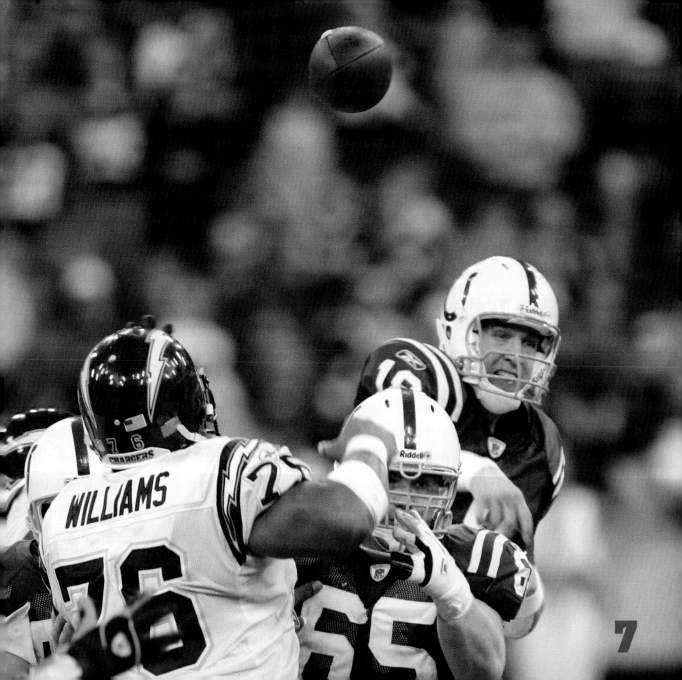

7

Peyton's dad was a pro quarterback too. He taught Peyton to throw a football.

Peyton's brother Eli is also a quarterback. He plays for the New York Giants.

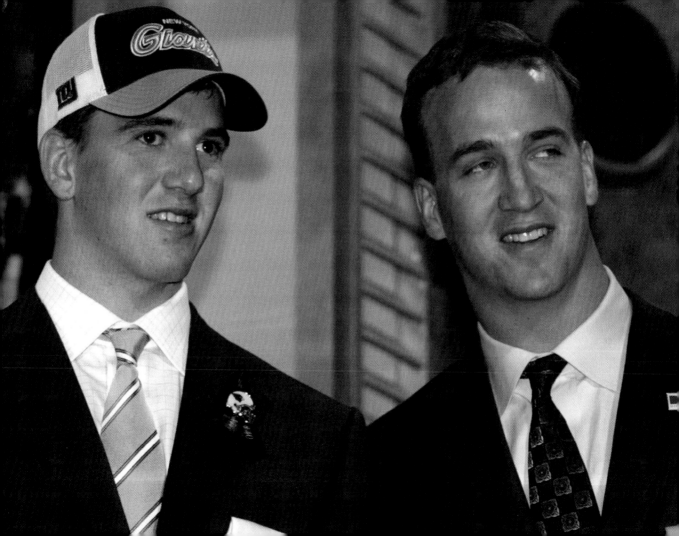

Peyton was a quarterback in college. He made the most passes ever at his college.

13

Peyton won a national football award in his last year of college. His shirt is hanging at the college.

In 1998, Peyton Manning was the first player picked by a pro football team.

17

Peyton was MVP in the 2005 Pro Bowl game. That means he was the best player in the game.

18

19

Peyton helps children and others in his community. He received an award for his good work.

Glossary

award (uh-WARD) A prize or honor given for something you have done.

college (KAH-lihj) A school you go to after high school.

pro (PROH) A person who plays a sport for money.

quarterback (KWOR-tuhr-bak) The player who throws the ball and leads the team.

touchdown (TUCH-down) A score made in football when a player carries or catches the ball over the other team's goal line.

Index

A
award, 14, 20

C
college, 12, 14
community, 20

D
dad, 8

E
Eli, 10

I
Indianapolis Colts, 4

M
MVP, 18

N
New York Giants, 10

P
passes, 6, 12
Pro Bowl, 18

T
touchdown, 6

Books and Web Sites

BOOKS:
Horn, Geoffrey M. *Peyton Manning*. Milwaukee, WI: Gareth Stevens Publishing, 2005.

Savage, Jeffrey. *Peyton Manning*. Minneapolis, MN: Lerner Publishing, 2004.

WEB SITES: Due to the changing nature of Internet links, PowerKids Press has developed an online list of Web sites related to the subject of this book. This site is updated regularly. Please use this link to access the list:
http://www.powerkidslinks.com/spsuper/manning/

Glossary

award (uh-WARD) A prize or honor given for something you have done.

college (KAH-lihj) A school you go to after high school.

pro (PROH) A person who plays a sport for money.

quarterback (KWOR-tuhr-bak) The player who throws the ball and leads the team.

touchdown (TUCH-down) A score made in football when a player carries or catches the ball over the other team's goal line.